RIS RASCHKA

meow

 Greenwillow Books, *An Imprint of* HarperCollins*Publishers*

Watercolor was used to prepare the full-color art and text.

Library of Congress Cataloging-in-Publication Data is available.

ISBN 978-0-06-304935-2 (hardback)

First Edition

22 23 24 25 26 RTLO 10 9 8 7 6 5 4 3 2 1

Greenwillow Books

for
Apollo

me

me

Ow?

me

ew

m m m

m M

eee

marigold?

I'm sorry.

ow

me

me

yow

meow